The Magical Music Box

... introducing Princess Plié & Friends!

Mary Dressendofer & Cathy Vigliotti

Brought to you by Dancers Pointe™

ISBN:
Softcover   978-1-5035-1353-2
Hardcover   978-1-5035-1354-9
EBook   978-1-5035-1355-6

Printed in the United States of America by BookMasters, Inc
Ashland OH

September 2015
Rev. date: 09/10/2015

To order additional copies of this book, contact:
Xlibris
1-888-795-4274
www.Xlibris.com
Orders@Xlibris.com

Character Creators & Music Lyrics: Mary Dressendofer & Cathy Vigliotti
Creative Designer: Dana Vigliotti
Music Composition and additional lyrics:
Little Rockers, LLC
Vocalist: Ava Rose Dressendofer
Princess Plie © and friends is brought to you by Dancers Pointe™

The Magical Music Box

Mary Dressendofer & Cathy Vigliotti
Brought to you by Dancers Pointe™

Illustrations By: Kenny Estrella and Dana Vigliotti

Dedication

This book is dedicated to John, Ava, Laura, Jim, Dana, Ferdinando, Irma, Dolly and Uncle Jr. for your unconditional love and continued support.

Hi! What's your name?

Are you ready to dance with me?!

I'm Princess Plié

I dance all day

With Passé, Bourrée and tiny Piqué

With tutu in hand, we'll dance through the land

Painting rainbows, making friendships,
we'll dance hand in hand.

8

I'm Princess Plié, I put on my shoes

I warm up with stretching and then start to move

I light up the room with rhythm and grace

Turning and leaping, a smile on my face!

Dancing, dancing, come join the fun

With me and all of my friends...

Dancing, dancing, come join the fun

Until the music ends...

I'm Princess Plié, so nice to meet you

I hope you love dancing as much as I do...

We'll practice our steps, and bend at the barre

What a magical, wonderful world where we are!

Dancing, dancing, come join the fun

With me and all of my friends...

Dancing, dancing, come join the fun

Until the music ends...

I'm Princess Plié, so nice to meet you!

I hope you love dancing as much as I do...

We'll practice our steps, and bend at the barre

What a magical, wonderful world where we are!

Come dance with me now!

Ready everyone?

Plié, relevé

Plié, relevé

Plié, straight knees, tendu,

Coupé

Pas de Bourrée

Pas de Bourrée

Step and curtsy that's our dance for today...

Come on let's do it again...

Plié, relevé

Plié, relevé

Plié, straight knees, tendu,

Coupé

Pas de Bourrée

Pas de Bourrée

Step and curtsy that's our dance for today...

Great Job Everybody!